Robin Hood
and his
Miserable Men

Other *Young Puffin Read It Yourself* titles

DICK KING-SMITH

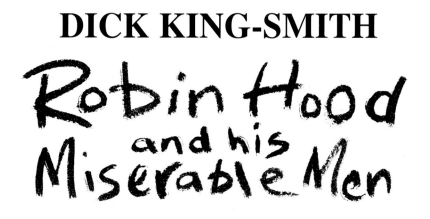

ILLUSTRATED BY
JOHN EASTWOOD

PUFFIN BOOKS

PUFFIN BOOKS

Published by the Penguin Group
Penguin Books Ltd, 27 Wrights Lane, London W8 5TZ, England
Penguin Putnam Inc., 375 Hudson Street, New York, New York 10014, USA
Penguin Books Australia Ltd, Ringwood, Victoria, Australia
Penguin Books Canada Ltd, 10 Alcorn Avenue, Toronto, Ontario, Canada M4V 3B2
Penguin Books (NZ) Ltd, Private Bag 102902, NSMC, Auckland, New Zealand

On the World Wide Web: www.penguin.com

Penguin Books Ltd, Registered Offices: Harmondsworth, Middlesex, England

First published in *The Topsy-Turvy Storybook* by Victor Gollancz Ltd 1992
Published in Puffin Books 1998
5 7 9 10 8 6 4

Printed in Hong Kong by Wing King Tong

British Library Cataloguing in Publication Data
A CIP catalogue record for this book is available from the British Library

ISBN 0–141–30035–3

SNOW-WHITE

There was once a King whose wife gave birth to a baby daughter.

Unfortunately the poor woman then died, so that the baby, whose name was Snow-White, was left motherless.

She was called Snow-White because she was a pasty-faced baby, with no hint of colour in her cheeks.

After some years the King married again. The new Queen was enormously fat and proud of it, and she took an immediate dislike to Snow-White who was by now a very plump child and putting on weight at quite a rate.

Angrily the Queen stood in front of her mirror (a magic one, by the way) and said:

> "Mirror, mirror on the wall,
> Who is the fattest one of all?"

and the mirror (which always told the truth) replied:

"Lady Queen, you are the fattest one of all."

But as time passed, Snow-White grew not only taller but thicker and wider as well, and when the Queen next asked the mirror:

"Mirror, mirror on the wall,
Who is the fattest one of all?"

the mirror replied:

"To say it's you would not be right.
The fattest one is now Snow-White."

At this Snow-White's wicked stepmother became so angry that she ordered her

6

huntsman to take Snow-White out into the
forest and there do away with her.

"She's as fat as a pig," she said, "so you can
kill her, and then bring me back her lungs and
her liver. I'll have 'em for supper."

But out in the forest the huntsman couldn't
bring himself to shove his knife through all
those layers of blubber, so he told Snow-White
to get lost. Then he caught a real pig, a wild
forest hog, and killed it, and took its lungs and
liver back to the Queen.

She ordered them to be fried, and then she

covered them with dollops of blood-red tomato sauce and scoffed the lot. Afterwards she got upon the scales and saw with pleasure that she had gained a couple of pounds.

Snow-White, meanwhile, had stumbled upon a funny little house in the depths of the forest. Its front door was much too small for a big fat girl like her and she broke it off its hinges while getting in. Inside was a little table with seven little plates of food and seven little mugs of drink.

As usual, Snow-White was hungry, so she sat down, smashing the seven little chairs one after another, and ate all the food and drank all the drink. Then she felt sleepy, so she pushed together all the seven little beds that were ranged along one wall, and lay down on them. They all broke.

After dark the seven dwarfs whose house this was returned from their work as miners, and lit seven little lamps, and saw what had happened.

"The front door's bust," said the first dwarf.

"So are all our chairs," said the second dwarf.

"And all our food's gone," said the third.

"And all our drink," said the fourth.

"And all our beds are broken," said the fifth.

"Thanks to that great fat lump of a girl who's sleeping on them," said the sixth.

"Come on, boys," said the seventh dwarf. "Let's teach her a lesson."

So the seven dwarfs grabbed hold of Snow-White with their fourteen little hands, and between them dragged her away (for though

they were small, they were strong), and dumped her down an old mineshaft.

Luckily there were some pools of water at the bottom of the shaft, otherwise Snow-White would have died of thirst, but there was nothing to eat and so she rapidly became much thinner.

Thus it was that when the Queen next addressed her magic mirror, saying as usual:

"Mirror, mirror on the wall,
Who is the fattest one of all?"

the mirror replied:

"You are the fattest one around,
For now Snow-White is underground."

Then the Queen was sure Snow-White was dead.

"Not that I doubted it," she said to herself. "She wouldn't have got far without her lungs and her liver."

But in fact before long Snow-White was rescued.

A young Prince, hunting in the forest, heard her faint cries for help from the bottom of the mineshaft. He let down a rope and pulled her up – fairly easily for now she was quite a pretty

shape. And the Prince fell in love with her on the spot as princes do, and took her home, and married her.

He would have done better to wait a bit, because now Snow-White was so hungry that she spent every hour of the day eating. Soon she was even fatter than she had ever been, and the poor Prince found himself with a pasty-faced wife who thought of nothing but food and was disgustingly greedy.

Meanwhile, back at the palace, the Queen could not break herself of the habit of consulting the magic mirror.

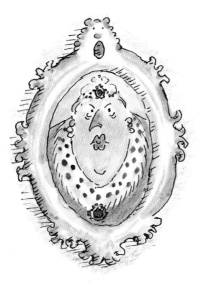

"Mirror, mirror on the wall,
Who is the fattest one of all?"

she asked with a smug smile on her face.
But the mirror replied:

"Snow-White's the fattest. She's not dead
But to a handsome Prince is wed.
She's fatter than she's ever been,
So eat your heart out, Lady Queen."

On hearing these words, Snow-White's wicked
stepmother promptly died of a broken heart.
As for Snow-White and her handsome
Prince, they both lived unhappily ever after.

I LOVE LITTLE PUSSY

I hate little pussy
For making me sneeze.
Whenever she's near me
I sniff and I wheeze.

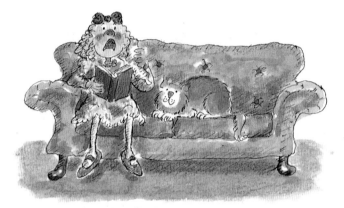

So I shoo her away
And I shout at her "Scat!"
I'm allergic to pussy,
The hairy old cat.

THE FROG KING

Once there was a Princess (beautiful of course) whose favourite toy was a ball (a gold one, naturally) which (because I suppose she couldn't think of anything better to do) she liked to play with by throwing it up into the air and catching it again.

One day she was doing this beside a well, when she missed (butterfingers) and the ball dropped into the well and sank.

Whereupon (being a thoroughly spoiled little miss) she began to stamp her feet and bawl her eyes out.

Just then a croaky voice (yes, you've guessed, it was a frog) said, "Oi, you! Why are you making all that fuss?"

"I dropped my, boo-hoo, gold ball into the, boo-hoo, well," sobbed the Princess.

"Well, what will you, ribbit-ribbit, give me if I,

ribbit-ribbit, fetch it out for you?" said the frog.

"Anything you like!" cried the Princess. "My jewels, my pearls, my dresses – anything."

"No fear," said the frog. "That's not my scene. But if you will love me, and let me sit beside you at table and eat off your golden plate and drink from your mug, then I'll go down and fetch your rotten old ball."

The frog, you see, (you knew it all the time, didn't you?) was actually a handsome young King who'd got on the wrong side of a witch. Only the kindness of a Princess could change him back again.

The Princess dried her tears.

"OK, frog," she said. "It's a deal."

So the Frog King dived down into the well and fetched the gold ball. Then the Princess carried him home.

Once inside the palace the Princess took the Frog King straight down to the kitchens. Here she gave orders to the Head Cook. Then she came out, without the Frog King.

When all the other members of her family came into the banqueting hall for supper that evening, the Princess had already started her meal (by the way, I forgot to tell you she was a French Princess).

The others looked at what was on the Princess's golden plate.

"*Qu'est-ce que tu manges?*" they asked.

("What are you eating?")

And the Princess replied:

"*Les cuisses de grenouille.*"

("Frog's legs.")

ROCK-A-BYE, BABY

Rock-a-bye, baby, on the tree top.
Oh, that the horrible baby would stop!
The ugly great creature's so heavy and fat
The poor little tree's going to fall over flat.

RING-A-RING O' ROSES

Ring-a-ring o' roses,
You've all got runny noses.
Goodness, how I loathe 'em.
Don't you ever blow them?
Atishoo! Atishoo!
Is all I hear all day.
I don't want your sniffly colds.
Sneeze the other way.

ROBIN HOOD AND HIS MISERABLE MEN

Long long ago, in Sherwood Forest in the county of Nottinghamshire, there lived a man who was known as Robin Hood, probably because he liked robin people.

He had a wife called Maid Marian, probably

because Robin made her keen on marian him.

Maid Marian had a great many sisters, so that Robin acquired a whole lot of brothers-in-law, who became known as the Inlaws, and a miserable lot of fellows they were.

You can't blame them really, because they had no roof over their heads in Sherwood Forest and most of the time it rained, and often it was bitterly cold, except sometimes in summertime and even then the trees were so thick they didn't see much of the sun.

What's more, they didn't have much to eat except for nuts and berries, because although the forest was full of deer, all the Inlaws were such rotten shots. They shot at the deer like mad with their longbows, but though the arrows flew everywhere, into bushes and tree trunks and sometimes into other Inlaws, they hardly ever hit a deer.

Actually Robin Hood was the worst bowman of them all. A skinny weakly little chap, he could never draw the bowstring tight enough to send the arrow any distance.

Even when someone did manage to kill a deer, usually either a very young or a very

old one, most of the band didn't get much of it, because two of the Inlaws got the lion's share.

One was a giant of a man called Little John, and the other was a very fat and greedy priest named Friar Tuck. Little John used to biff the other Inlaws with a great pole called a quarter-staff to keep them away, and then he and Friar Tuck would gorge themselves while Robin Hood and his Miserable Men stood around in the rain, hoping for scraps.

Poor old Robin Hood, he led a wretched life. Most of the time he was wet and cold and hungry. None of his Miserable Men, like Will Scarlet or Allan A'Dale or Much the miller's son, thought anything of him. Little John and Friar Tuck ate all the grub. Maid Marian gave him a hard time.

And finally the Sheriff of Nottingham and his men were for ever chasing about in the forest trying to catch Robin Hood. They needn't really have bothered, because he was a most unsuccessful robber. He had the idea, you see, that it was his mission in life to rob the poor to feed the rich, but of course the poor people he stole from never had two pennies to rub together.

Saddest of all was his end.

As he lay dying (of exposure, starvation, double pneumonia and a broken heart), he said to Maid Marian, "Bring me my bow."

"Whatever for?" she said.

"I will shoot an arrow," said Robin Hood, "and wherever it falls, there bury me."

All the Miserable Men, the whole band of Inlaws, were standing around, and they heard these words.

"One thing's sure," said Will Scarlet. "We shan't have far to carry him."

"Too true," said Allan A'Dale. "He never could shoot any distance."

"And he certainly won't be able to now," said Much the miller's son.

"I might as well dig the grave right next to him," said Little John, and so he did.

Then the Inlaws helped poor old Robin fit an arrow to his bowstring.

He pulled it feebly and the arrow plopped straight into the grave.

Exhausted by the effort, Robin Hood died.

"Bless him," said Friar Tuck, as they tipped the body in.

Little John leaned on his quarterstaff and looked down reflectively at the skinny little corpse.

"Poor old chap," he said. "He never amounted to anything when he was alive. Why don't we make sure he does now that he's dead?"

"What d'you mean?" asked the other Inlaws.

"Well," said Little John, "let's spread the story that Robin Hood was really a hero – a marvellous bowman, a wonderful fighter feared by all his enemies, especially the Sheriff of Nottingham, and loved and admired by all his Miserable Men."

"Merry Men would be better," said Friar Tuck.

"And if we tell enough people," went on Little John, "then in time everyone will come to believe that was what Robin Hood was really like."

So that's what they did.

MARY, MARY

Mary, Mary, quite contrary,
How does your garden grow?
It's nothing to do
With nosy old you,
So mind your own business and go.

THE SLEEPING BEAUTY

Everyone knows the story of the Sleeping
Princess.

How twelve jolly nice fairies were invited to
her christening, but the thirteenth, a smelly
old toe-rag, wasn't. And how the old toe-rag
was niggled at not being asked, and so
promised that, at the age of fifteen, the
Princess would prick her finger with a needle
and die.

And how the twelfth (jolly nice) fairy said,
"No, she won't, she'll just fall into a deep sleep
for a hundred years."

Well, you'd have thought the Princess would
have had the sense to steer clear of needles,
but no, at the age of fifteen the silly creature
had to come across an aged woman (any fool
should have known it was the old toe-rag) and
have a go on her spinning-wheel, and prick

her finger, and KER-ZONK! she was out like
a light.

Everyone knows too that the inhabitants of
the Palace also fell asleep at that precise
moment. The King, the Queen, the courtiers,
the servants, the animals – every one of them
dropped off, no matter what they were doing.

Cooks stirring soup, serving-wenches
sweeping floors, gardeners digging, bakers
baking, butlers butling, flunkeys flunking,
ostlers ostling, and turnspits turning spits –
each fell fast asleep in the middle of whatever

he or she was doing. The Queen's little pet dog
in fact had his leg cocked, all ready to sprinkle
the white-stockinged leg of the Chamberlain of
the Royal Household, but both were instantly in
slumberland before any damage could be done.

Everyone knows all this stuff, but what
no one knows is exactly what happened a
hundred years later.

I don't mean the bit about a Prince hearing
the story of the Sleeping Beauty, and making

his way through the terrible thorn-hedge that had grown up around the Palace. Nor the part where he finds all the inhabitants snoring their heads off.

I mean when he actually reached the Princess's bedchamber, and stared down at her sleeping figure and saw how beautiful she was. OK so he kissed her and she woke up.

And so did the King and the Queen and all the court, and the cooks started stirring again, the serving-wenches swept, the gardeners dug, the bakers baked, the butlers butled, the flunkeys flunked, the ostlers ostled, and the turnspits turned their spits.

And the Queen's little pet dog made a pretty design all down the Chamberlain of the Royal Household's white-stockinged leg.

But up in the bedchamber the Princess gave the Prince one heck of a smack in the face.

"I don't know who you think you are," she said, "but you've got a flipping nerve, barging into a girl's room and waking her up. I need my beauty sleep."

"But . . . but . . . but," stammered the Prince, "I thought you wanted waking up. You've been asleep for a hundred years."

"A hundred years!" said the Princess. "You must be joking! What d'you think this is – a fairy story?"